Timeless Fairy T

Cinderella

AWARD PUBLICATIONS LIMITED

Once upon a time there was a rich merchant who lived with his only daughter. His wife had died, but after some time he had married again, hoping that his new wife and her two daughters would take care of his only child while he was working.

"You can forget your name," the sisters said spitefully once they were alone with the merchant's daughter. "From now on, we're going to call you Cinderella! Your place is in the kitchen, among the cinders."

So Cinderella became a servant in the l ouse, cleaning and washing all day long. And nev she get a word of thanks from anyone.

Usually the two sisters were mean and ba tempered, but when an invitation came one day for a ball at the Royal Palace, they rushed into the kitchen to tell Cinderella all about it.

Splendid new gowns were ordered and when they arrived, Cinderella had to help with the fittings. How she longed to go to the ball herself! But when she dared speak about it, her stepsisters only laughed at her. "How can you go to the ball, in those rags?" they teased.

Cinderella was left all alone in the kitchen, wishing with all her heart she could go to the ball. Suddenly, there was a flash of light and a strange old lady appeared. In her hand was a silver wand.

"I am your very own Fairy Godmother," she said in a gentle voice, "and I can make your dreams come true!"

"If it is your wish to go to the Royal Ball, child, then so you shall," she smiled.

"But I don't have a dress to wear," said Cinderella, "or a coach to get to the palace."

"Let's go into the garden, and we will see what can be done," said the Fairy Godmother.

First, she found a round, yellow pumpkin and touched it with her wand. It changed at once into a splendid coach! The fairy turned to Cinderella, smiling. “This coach will take you to the ball,” she said. “Did I not tell you that I could make wishes come true? Now, fetch me the big mousetrap I saw near the door.”

Cinderella gasped as her Godmother changed the two white mice in the trap into a pair of handsome, white horses. Then a long-whiskered rat was turned into a fat, jolly coachman. And at the touch of the magic wand, a pair of lizards became two very smart footmen in uniform.

Cinderella hung her head sadly when the fairy told her that her coach was waiting. “How can I go to the ball in rags?” she cried.

Her Godmother winked and with the wave of her wand, she changed Cinders’ tatty old dress into a beautiful gown and her worn-out shoes into a pair of dainty glass slippers.

“Now you are ready to go to the ball,” she said. “But there is one thing you must remember…”

“You must leave before the clock strikes twelve. If you do not, your gown will change back to rags, your coach into a pumpkin, and all will be as it once was!”

Cinderella thanked the fairy for all her magic, stepped into the coach and was driven off into the moonlit night.

When she arrived at the palace, and stepped into the grand ballroom, all the lords and ladies stared in amazement at the unknown guest.

"Such a beauty!" said one of the ladies.

"And what a magnificent dress!" gasped another.

As soon as the Prince saw Cinderella, he fell instantly in love. He did not know her name, but his heart was captivated and he asked her to dance. As light as a butterfly in the Prince's arms, she seemed to float around the room.

"Who can she be?" one Ugly Sister whispered. "She must be a Princess from a faraway land; she surely does not live in these parts."

"There is certainly no one in the room quite so lovely," replied the other. "The Prince will never notice us now," she added, sadly.

All around the glittering ballroom the lords and ladies were puzzling over the beautiful stranger. Not one of them recognised her at all.

The Prince was so enchanted with the mysterious Cinderella that he would dance with no one else.

But Cinderella was so shy that she could not speak and he thought she must indeed be a Princess.

Cinderella was having such a wonderful time that she forgot all about the fairy's warning – until suddenly she heard the palace clock begin to strike midnight.

Without a word of farewell to the Prince, she fled from the ballroom down the great marble staircase.

As she ran, one of her glass slippers fell off, but she did not dare stop to pick it up.

At the last stroke of twelve,
the wonderful ball gown vanished and Cinderella was back in her old, ragged dress.

There was no golden coach waiting to carry her home… No jolly coachman to greet her before urging his white horses into a trot… And no smart footmen… They had all completely vanished!

"If only I had remembered the fairy's words!" Cinderella sighed.

As she hurried home through the dark night, all that remained of the Fairy Godmother's magic was the large yellow pumpkin by the roadside, and two little mice scampering about. Darting away into the bushes was a fat, brown rat with long whiskers, while two, green lizards slipped safely under a stone.

Dawn was beginning to break as Cinderella fell asleep in her corner of the kitchen, to dream of her wonderful evening.

The next morning, the Ugly Sisters couldn't stop talking about the ball, and the lovely Princess who had captured the Prince's heart. Cinderella was busy dusting and sweeping but she could not help smiling to herself as she heard what they had to say about the beautiful Princess.

"We mustn't blame the Prince for not dancing with us," they said at last. "She was so beautiful."

Later that day, there was great excitement in the town. The Prince had sent a courtier out with a page boy carrying the glass slipper that Cinderella had dropped.

"His Royal Highness, the Prince, wishes to marry the lady who can wear the glass slipper that was found last night at the palace," the courtier told the townspeople.

The courtier and the page boy visited every house in the town. At last, they came to the house where the Ugly Sisters lived.

"I am sure that slipper will fit my foot!" cried one sister. But her foot was much too big and the other sister laughed.

"Now let me try," she exclaimed. But no matter how she pushed and pulled, the slipper would not go on!

The courtier asked if any other young ladies lived in the house. “Only the servant girl, Cinderella!” they replied.

“Then fetch her here,” commanded the courtier. “She must be allowed to try on the glass slipper.”

And, to the amazement of everyone watching, the beautiful glass slipper fitted Cinderella’s tiny foot perfectly.

The Ugly sisters simply could not believe their eyes! They insisted there must be a mistake and ordered Cinderella back to the kitchen. But before she could obey, the kind Fairy Godmother appeared and touched Cinderella with her magic wand, changing her back into the lovely Princess who had danced at the ball.

Soon she was reunited with the Prince, who was overjoyed to see Cinderella again.

This time, the Prince took Cinderella's hand and begged her to marry him. She immediately agreed, and plans for the wedding were made.

The Ugly Sisters tried their best to pretend that they were full of joy at Cinderella's new-found happiness. And Cinderella, with her kind and forgiving heart, made sure that they received a special invitation to the wedding!

THE END